Red
and the Egg Pie

Red
and the Egg Pie

Written by Donna Gingery

Illustrated by Letizia Rizzo

ARPress
45 Dan Road Suite 5
Canton MA 02021
Hotline: 1(888) 821-0229
Fax: 1(508) 545-7580

Ordering Information:
Quantity sales. Special discounts are available on quantity purchases by corporations, associations, and others. For details, contact the publisher at the address above.

Printed in the United States of America.

ISBN-13: Softcover   979-8-89676-171-6
          eBook   979-8-89676-172-3

Library of Congress Control Number: 2025907423

Good morning, rise and shine!

My name is Red.

Want to know how I got my name?

Well, when I was born, I was so red they started calling me Red, ha ha ha.

This is my sister, Kitty. She loves to read.

"Good morning, Kitty!"

My granny and I are the best of friends.
She wakes me up every morning, saying,
"Good morning, rise and shine!"

I can always smell the coffee and
bacon—it sure makes me hungry.

At night, while drinking eggnog, we talk about anything that comes to our minds.

I just know she is the smartest granny in the whole wide world.

Granny always tells me: "Red, don't you
go over to people's houses begging."

And I always say, "Granny, I don't beg. They say,
'Red, you want some food?' and I say yes."

"Well, stop saying yes."

"Okay, Granny."

One day, I went next door
to my best friend's house.

Her granny is so nice.

She says, "Red, you want some of this good ol' pie?" Hum . . .

"No thanks, I'm not hungry."

In my mind, I remember what my granny said: Stop eating at everyone's house in the neighborhood.

But look at that pie!

I'm smelling that good ol' pie and it's my best friend's granny. I'm thinking, how can I resist?

I will just take a little bite.

She cuts a piece of the
pie and my mouth begins
to water and I get so excited!

She puts the pie on a plate and I put a fork
into the pie. My mouth begins to say yum,
yum, yum. I open my mouth, it touches my
tongue, and the pie tastes bad to me.

Yuck!

I chew the piece of pie that is in my mouth and say to my friend's granny that I have to go home.

Her granny says, "You want to take the pie home?"

14

"Oh no, mam, I'm not feeling well."

I run out the house, trying to find a place
to spit the pie out.

Uh oh, my granny is looking
out of the window and I can hear
her say, "Red, come here."

"Mam?"

"Come here."

"Yes, mam."

"What are you doing?"

"Nothing."

"Red."

"Mam?"

"What were you doing next door?"

I want to lie, but I know if I did Granny would find out, and then I would get in more trouble. So I say, "Granny, I had a piece of my friend's granny's egg pie."

Granny says, "Red, the next time you eat somebody else's egg pie, I'm gonna make you lay an egg!"

- Evaluate the author's purpose by completing this sentence: I think the author wrote this book to…

- Who does Red remind you of?

- Who does Red's sister, Kitty remind you of?

- Who does Red's granny remind you of?

- Make a prediction of what Red will do the next time she visits her neighbor's house.

- Write a new ending to the story.

- Make stick puppets of the main characters and retell the story using the puppets.

Donna Gingery was born in Selma, Alabama, in the 1960s. She is a survivor because she was a premature baby and was not expected to live. Donna says her life in elementary through high school was not very pleasant. She was diagnosed with a learning disability and struggled with reading and writing. Donna's high school counselor told her that she would never make it in college—but today Donna has a bachelor's degree in theater, a master's degree in educational leadership, and a K-12 administration license. She credits a teacher she had for counteracting what her high school counselor told her. This teacher told Donna that she was smart and learned differently. She told Donna to never allow anyone to tell her otherwise. Her words helped Donna become the educator she is today.

Her love for storytelling started at a very young age. Donna has always had a big imagination. It was her imagination that helped her get through school and other adversities in her life. When Donna was growing up, if someone would ask her a question, she would always answer with some elaborate story. Every night at bedtime, Donna's sister would ask her to tell her a story. If Donna refused to tell a story, her sister would get very upset. This is when Donna realized her love for storytelling. Donna is a sister, a wife, a mother, a grandmother, and a friend to many. She lives in Prior Lake, Minnesota, with her husband.